CW00665415

Contents

*G = gold; P = platinum; ( ) = the line must be played but cannot be assessed for a Medal.

Levels in bold type indicate that the piece is for mixed saxophones. In each of these cases, the instrumentation is given at the start of the piece. Every other piece can be played either on E flat saxophones or on B flat saxophones.

Alexander the Goat

Beverley Calland

AB 3142

Baroque Improvisation

Alan Haughton

The Golden Vanity

Trad. English arr. Nicholas Hare

AB 3142

to Lorenzo

Argentina

Jonathan Leathwood

AB 3142

Bobby Dazzler

Mike Hall

AB 3142

Red Car

Mark Lockheart

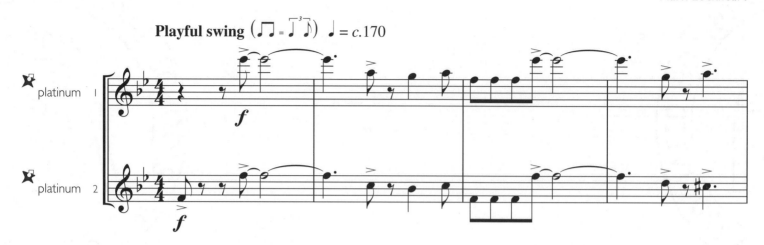

AB 3142

Figaro's March

(Aria 'Non più andrai') from *The Marriage of Figaro*

Mozart arr. Paul Harris

AB 3142

It's Your Move!

Robert Tucker

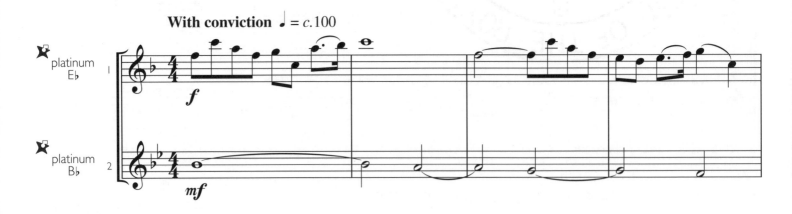

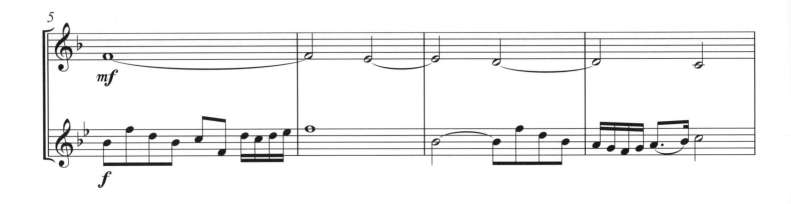

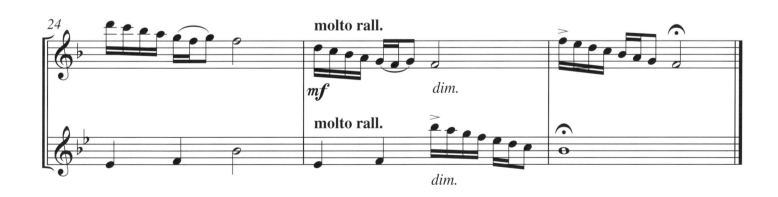

Rag-a-muffin

Alan Haughton

AB 3142

The Death of Queen Jane

Trad. English arr. Jonathan Leathwood

AB 3142

Gone Fishin'

Richard Ingham

Bending the note in bar 13 is optional for the Medal.

AB 3142

Kaleidoscopic

Paul Harris

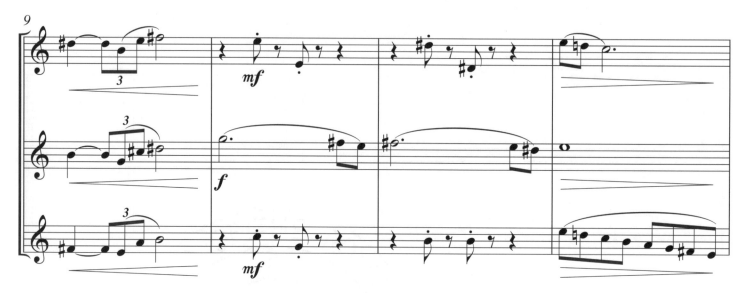

AB 3142

Reel Time

Richard Ingham

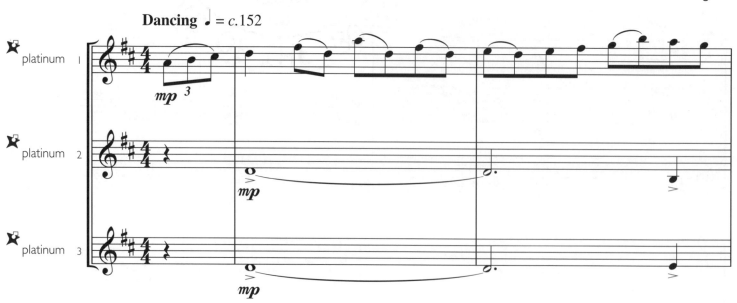

AB 3142

Parade of the Dragonflies

Martin Ellerby

Piece for Musical Clock

Haydn arr. Nicholas Hare

Awesome Rag

Chris Allen

Safaria

Nigel Wood

AB 3142

Bending the note in bar 39 is optional for the Medal.

AB 3142